A JUST ONE MORE BOOK
Just For You

Squirrel's Thanksgiving Surprise

by Valerie Tripp

Illustrated by Sandra Cox Kalthoff

Developed by The Hampton-Brown Company, Inc.

 CHILDRENS PRESS ®

CHICAGO

Word List

Give children books they can read by themselves, and they'll alway ask for JUST ONE MORE. This book is written with 87 of the most basic words in our language, all repeated in an appealing rhythm and rhyme.

a	find(s)	many	see
all	first	me	she
and	fly	more	so
are	for	mouse	some
around	found	my	squirrel
as	friends		surprise
at		need	
	ground	nice	thank
bag		no	Thanksgiving
bounce	happy	nut(s)	that
breaks	has		the
bring	have	of	them
but	help	oh	thing
	her	on	time
chipmunk		one('s)	to
come	I	or	too
couldn't	in		tree
	is	picks	
day	it	plenty	up
do(n't)			us
	just	rabbit	
each		raccoon	want
empty	last	roll	way
every	let	runs	what
	look(s)		will
fall	long	secret	
field			you

Library of Congress Cataloging-in-Publication Data
Tripp, Valerie, 1951-
   Squirrel's Thanksgiving Surprise / by Valerie Tripp ; Sandra Cox Kalthoff, illustrator.
     p.   cm. — (A Just one more book just for you)
    Summary: When Squirrel collects all the nuts, the other animals think her greedy until they discover she needed them for a Thanksgiving surprise.
  ISBN 0-516-01568-0
  [1. Squirrels—Fiction. 2. Animals— Fiction. 3. Thanksgiving Day—Fiction.] I. Kalthoff, Sandra Cox, ill. II. Title. III. Series.
PZ7.T7363Th   1988   87-35518
[E]—dc19   CIP
                                 AC

Squirrel has a secret.
She has a way
to surprise all her friends
on Thanksgiving Day.

Squirrel looks in her nut bag.
Oh no! It is empty!

Squirrel has to find nuts.
She will need plenty!

Squirrel looks a long time.
At last!   She finds nuts!
As she picks up the last one,
Chipmunk runs up.

I want that nut
and you want it, too.
But you found it first,
so that one's for you.

Thank you, Chipmunk!

Squirrel looks a long time.
At last!   Some more nuts!
As she picks up the last one,
Raccoon runs up.

I want that nut
and you want it, too.
But you found it first,
so that one's for you.

Thank you, Raccoon!

Squirrel looks a long time.
At last!   Some more nuts!
As she picks up the last one,
Rabbit runs up.

12

I want that nut
and you want it, too.
But you found it first,
so that one's for you.

Thank you, Rabbit!

Squirrel looks a long time.

At last!   Some more nuts!

As she picks up the last one,

Field Mouse runs up.

I want that nut
and you want it, too.
But you found it first,
so that one's for you.

Thank you, Field Mouse!

But!

JUST ONE MORE nut

is one nut

too many...

Squirrel's bag breaks!
Nuts fall all around.
Nuts fly!   Nuts roll!
Nuts bounce to the ground!

Do you need them,
every one?
Couldn't you let
us have some?

No! I need them!
Come and see!
Help me bring them
to my tree.

Happy Thanksgiving

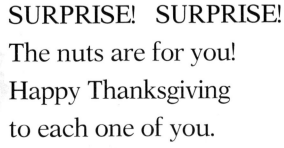

SURPRISE! SURPRISE!
The nuts are for you!
Happy Thanksgiving
to each one of you.

all my friends!

What a surprise!
What a nice thing to do!
Happy Thanksgiving!
And, Squirrel…

to all my fr___d__!

THANK YOU!